COFFEE & KITTENS

A SMALL TOWN SHIFTER AGE GAP ROMANCES

CLAIMED

CHRISTINA MATTINGLY

Copyright © 2024 by Christina Mattingly

All rights reserved.

No part of this publication may be reproduced, distributed, or transmitted in any form or by any means, including photocopying, recording, or other electronic or mechanical methods, without the prior written permission of the publisher, except as permitted by U.S. copyright law. For permission requests, contact christinamattinglywrites@gmail.com.

The story, all names, characters, and incidents portrayed in this production are fictitious. No identification with actual persons (living or deceased), places, buildings, and products is intended or should be inferred.

To all the good girls who want a grumpy shifter that remembers your coffee order and kneels to eat your pussy like you're his full moon dessert... this one's for you.

1

JARED

Jared stumbled down to the coffee shop, grumbling. His usual opener Zachary was 'sick' - which meant that he'd probably had indulged in too much sex and alcohol on the full moon. Jared had assured him he didn't need to work the morning after the full moon, but Zachary had insisted that he needed the money.

He didn't need the money bad enough to show up to work, Jared's wolf pointed out with a huff.

He's young, it happens. Jared thought back as he went through the motions of setting everything up in a hurry.

His first customer was one of the local paramedics, coming in for his shift's usual coffee order.

"Who's on?" Jared asked without greeting.

"Just picking up for me, Ryder, and Brian," Blake said.

"You got it," Jared replied, selecting their usual orders from a special menu he'd setup for his regulars back when he first hired someone to help him in the coffee shop.

When his regulars came in, Jared wanted a smoother experience so he had one of the local tech-savvy fae kids from the high school come build him an app that connected to a database. Regular customers got a two-sided rewards card, one to scan to add an order to their account so they got points, the other to scan to automatically populate their favorite drink order. People like Blake who frequently came in and ordered coffee for an entire shift got a separate card that would pull up the members of their shift, so the cashier on duty just had to click the right checkboxes for names and the orders were done.

"Hey, add in something for the Chief, too," Blake said, glancing at his phone.

"Yup," Jared said, tapping his screen to add the coffee to the order and send the whole thing to the county's tab.

He was in the middle of making their drinks when the door chimed. He checked the date on his watch and realized he'd forgotten to send last month's invoice for the county. Cursing to himself, he made a mental note to do that as soon as the morning rush was over. He looked up and nodded in greeting to the EMS and Fire Chief's assistant, Lela.

"Morning Jared," she chirped.

"Lela," he said.

"How are you this morning?" she asked, offering him a timid smile.

"Fine," he said. "I'll be with you in a sec."

"Take your time," she said, looking at the menu as if she didn't get the same damned thing every time.

Jared huffed, his mind going to the invoice he needed to send. If Lela didn't take all fucking morning, he might be able to knock it out before other customers came in.

"I think I'll have, um..." she bit her red-lipstick painted bottom lip, her pretty face turned up to the board. He started ringing up her order and told her her total, and she looked hurt.

"Hey. I haven't ordered yet," she objected, her heavily made-up eyes moving from the board to give him a frustrated look he certainly didn't deserve. He was saving her time, she should be thanking him, not looking at him like he'd bitten her.

"You're getting a large coffee with whipped cream. No, we don't have any of your fancy coconut kind and I still don't have any cherries. Do you want a blueberry muffin or chocolate?"

"Maybe I don't want a muffin."

"You always get a muffin," he said, giving her a glare.

He was the one who rung her up practically every day and got it out of the case for her. He would know if she got a moon-cursed muffin or not every morning.

"I do not!" she objected.

"You're right," he said, rolling his eyes briefly. "Sometimes you don't get one and you're back an hour later because not having a muffin ruined your morning. So how about you save me the time ringing you up again it and you the time of walking back here in the cold and just get it now?"

"Um. Okay," she said, swallowing hard and fiddling with her keyring. "I'll take chocolate, I guess."

She paid and took her coffee and moved away, greeting Blake and making small talk while he filled her order. Blake waited until the door swung shut behind her, adding some milk to his coffee before he spoke.

"You're kind of a dick, you know that?"

"She's always acting like she doesn't know what she wants when orders the same thing every fucking time. It's a waste of my time and hers," Jared said, clicking through his point of sale system to generate the county's invoice.

"She was trying to flirt with you," Blake pointed out.

That made Jared pause. There was no way she was trying to flirt with him. Women who wanted to flirt batted their eyelashes and crap. Plus, she was at least twenty years younger than he was. What business did she have flirting with him?

"If that's her trying to flirt, she sucks at it," Jared said, not in the mood to argue with Blake, who was obviously mistaken.

"You know, one of these days you're going to find a girl you like and you'll have to be nice to her," Blake pointed out, replacing the lid on his coffee.

"That's the exact reason I'm planning on staying single," Jared responded.

Jared got through the day with a steady stream of customers that kept him busy enough that he didn't think about the incident with Lela again. He locked up the shop and left out the back door, walking up the steps at the back of the building that led to the area he'd converted into his apartment a few years back. He made a salmon bisque for dinner, which he savored while listening to a true crime podcast.

Tomorrow was the full moon and he was restless. His body ached with the need to mate, but the last thing he wanted was some woman who would want to chit-chat and socialize.

Not for the first time he wished he was the sort of person who could see his full moon company as a means to an end, merely someone to enjoy the night with. He wasn't sure if it was because he'd been raised by two mothers and they'd instilled a hard respect for women, or maybe it was that he just really hated people, but the idea of meaningless sex just to get rid of the aching in his balls didn't appeal to him.

Rather than putting his energy into that, he pulled out the notebook if ideas he kept for ways to improve the coffee shop: new menu items to try, mostly. Normally he kept the notebook out of sight, but yesterday morning he'd left it out on a table as he'd enjoyed the quiet before the rush started. His tiny scrawl in black pen filled the top of the page.

The entries at the bottom of the page in pink ink read:

Coconut milk whipped cream
Cherries
Snowflake sprinkles for the holidays

With an eye roll, he eyed the loopy writing. She even dotted her i's with hearts like a fucking child. He thought back to the look on her face when he'd told her he knew her order this morning. He'd never had a customer *not* pleased he remembered their order.

"Flirting," he muttered, shaking his head. Blake was off his rocker. There was no way Lela had been flirting with him. She was half his age, for the moons' sake, and he'd certainly never given her any special attention.

But when he got in the water for his shower before he turned in for the night, he thought about how her eyes would light with pleasure if he got her stupid fancy crap. This was probably dumb. He'd try it once and never do it again when no one liked it.

When he got out of the shower he threw on clean clothes and trudged down the block to the grocery store. Grabbing the few things he needed, he grumbled the whole way home, going to bed. He fell asleep picturing how she would look when he had the things she suggested. Even if no one else would like them, maybe that would make up for hurting her feelings.

2

LELA

After the way Jared had spoken to her the other day, Lela had gone out and gotten herself one of those coffee machines for her office.

She'd tried to make conversation with the not-so-conversational Jared for the past few weeks. She'd even left a funny suggestion on his notebook with ideas for improvements, which had apparently just pissed him off because he'd been sort of a jerk about it.

Clearly, he was not interested in her at all and she should look elsewhere. She brushed off the disappointment and made herself a drink with her machine and mused that this would be cheaper in the long run, anyway, especially if she brought one of her mugs from home instead of buying a new one.

She added a squirt of the coconut based whipped cream, smiling at the result. Maybe she could learn to make the creamer designs like the fancy coffee places in Red River, even. Taking a few of the sprinkles she'd bought for herself, she tapped the bottle and let some of the little iridescent blue and white balls fall on top of her whipped cream.

Snapping a picture on her phone, she posted it just as her boss walked in, while she switched her coat for the thick office sweater she wore. Working in a building with lots of shifter men, she was always cold. Having fae blood meant not only did she not warm herself as well as a human would, but her body was even colder than the shifters who ran hot all year round.

"Morning," Jason said as he looked at her coffee machine, noticing the decal she made last night that looked like a caffeine molecule.

"Morning," she replied cheerily.

"I guess that means I'll have to get my own coffee from now on," he commented with a little wink. "Miss Linda thanks you."

"She still got you wearing the step counter?"

The alpha shifter's wife was concerned about his health, and had recently instituted a minimum step goal for him when he was spending so many long days at the office.

"Yup, the woman is gonna kill me trying to keep me healthy. Anything happen I need to know about?" He asked, nodding toward her computer where she was logged into her email.

"That shifter expert from the university still wants to come and do a study on the imprinted males, she's been very persistent."

"Alright, tell her I'll meet with her. Setup a call."

"She offered to come down and talk in person when I suggested you'd like that better, I have her on the schedule for Thursday."

Knowing her boss didn't like technology and wouldn't be satisfied with a phone call, when a recent graduate from the state university had asked permission to come study the males in Pinehurst who had imprinted, Lela had been happy to help.

Any woman who wanted to succeed in a male-dominated field who was supportive and kind to other women was an automatic friend to Lela and they'd worked hard to present her boss with the easiest way to get him to say yes to something most alphas would reject: letting an outsider come in and study a problem in their pack.

"Good, thank you Lela," he said, looking relieved.

"Everything else can wait until after your coffee," she promised.

"Well, good,"

"I can go get it for you," she offered, standing.

"No, no, let me get some of these infernal steps in," he said, walking away to set his briefcase down on his desk in his office and heading back out the front door.

SHE WAS in the middle of sending an email to the wolf pack council members on behalf of Jason when her phone rang.

"Hello?"

"Yes, is this Lela?"

"Yes, you've got me," Lela said.

"Oh, perfect! This is Sawyer, the volunteer coordinator from the Pinehurst vet and rescue? We spoke a few weeks ago?"

In a fit of loneliness, Lela had contacted the local rescue to apply to be a foster mom for cats.

"Oh, yeah, hi Sawyer."

"I have a kitten who is a little high-needs, she was found in a box the side of the highway and she'll need bottle feeding. Would you be interested and available?"

"Oh, well, let me ask my boss, but I don't think it will be a problem. Can I call you right back?"

"Sure!"

Lela stood up from her desk and walked to her boss' office.

"Do you have a second?" She asked, hovering in the doorway.

"I have a whole minute," her boss said, sighing as he put down a file folder. "What do you need?"

"I need permission to keep a cat in the office, temporarily," she said biting her lip. "He's a rescue. They found him in a box."

"A cat?"

"Well, he's a kitten actually, and he needs to be bottle fed, so if I volunteer as his foster I would need to be able to feed him."

"I'm sorry, I can't have a cat in the building, Miss Linda is allergic," her boss said with regret.

"Oh, no worries," she said. "I totally understand."

It hadn't occurred to her that her boss would say no, he was always so easygoing.

"If Linda wasn't allergic I wouldn't have an issue with it, sorry Lela."

"No, it's no problem" she assured.

Before she called Sawyer back, she texted her friend who lived across the hall, hoping she was awake.

LELA

Hey, wanna foster a kitten with me?

AMY

Totally!

LELA

I can't bring it to work with me, so maybe if you keep her when I'm at work, I can have her when I'm not at work, and we can figure out who wants her on the weekends?

AMY

ABSOLUTELY. I love cats!

LELA

Thank you! I figured you'd be down.

AMY

You know me. If it's an adventure, I'm in!
Plus, kitten cuddles!

Lela picked up her phone.

"Sawyer? Yes, this is Lela Thomas. I would love to foster a kitten."

3

JARED

Jared had bought her stupid coconut whipped cream and cherries and Lela hadn't been back since. He'd even taken the time to drive to forty five minutes into the city to get some fancy snowflake sprinkles, but she hadn't dropped by Code Brew for almost two weeks now. If he hadn't seen her walking by a few mornings he would have been worried that she was sick.

"Figures," Jared muttered.

He wondered if she was doing one of those diet things. The idea of her not loving her body made him clench his jaw. She'd been coming in damn near every morning for over a year, why else would she suddenly stop coming?

When his friend Fire Chief Jason Beckett walked in, Jared saw his opportunity to find out what was going on. Not that he cared, naturally, but he didn't want that whipped cream taking up space in his fridge if it wasn't going to be used. Who else would put that stuff in a coffee, for the moon's sake?

"I thought you had you normally have your minion get your coffee , chief."

"What's that?" asked, picking up his head to look at Jared as he removed his debit card from the machine.

"I thought you normally had your minion get your coffee," Jared said a little louder over the sound of Zachary grinding beans behind him.

"Meh, only because she was on her way here. She's got one of those machines in her office now."

Jared missed the brief smile that touched the Chief's lips as he closely watched his friend make his coffee. Jared's mood was suddenly darker than the dark roast coffee beans.

"You doing alright?" The Chief asked with a knowing smile that was lost on Jared, who was focused solely on making the Chief's coffee with a shot of espresso.

"Better than some, worse than others," Jared replied, putting Jason's coffee order on the fulfillment end of the counter.

"Mmhmm, haven't seen you at a pack meeting recently. Whatcha been doing with yourself? Got a new lady I don't know about?"

"Come on, you know there's no secrets in a town this small," Jared said with a little chuckle.

"You could be seeing a beauty from somewhere else," Jason said, shrugging, his eyes gleaming.

"Oh, get out of here, you old busybody, I'll settle down when I have time. Maybe I'll get lucky and take a leaf out of your book, hm?"

"How's that?"

"Maybe I'll meet the love off my life at work," Jared clarified as he wiped up the working counter.

"Maybe you already have," Jason countered.

"Gods, I hope not. The people I see in here most are you and your first responders. Now, I swing both ways, but most of them are too young and enthusiastic for me," Jared said, shuddering at the idea of a partner who was as young as some of the paramedics they hired these days.

The door chimed, announcing another customer coming in.

"Give me someone with a little more life experience," Jared continued, waving at Jason as he headed for the door.

Addressing the friendly middle-aged woman, he asked how he could help her.

"I'm not quite ready just yet," she said, looking at the menu above his head.

"Oh, hey Chief?" Jared called as the woman considered her menu choices.

"Yeah?" Jason asked, pausing with one foot out the door.

"Tell Lela I've got the cherries and the fancy whipped cream she wanted," Jared said.

That way she knew what she was missing. Those little home brew machines weren't nearly as good.

"I'll do that," Jason promised with a knowing twinkle in his eye.

After the morning rush had ended, Jared had Zachary handle the afternoon customers, leaving Jared free to restore order to the stock room. Zachary had accidentally made their usual order of supplies, just after Jared had, so they were trying to fit way too much into the small closet more suited to be a broom closet than a true storage area.

With a fair amount of cursing and a good deal of moving things around, he managed to fit everything inside in a mostly orderly manner that wouldn't get them in trouble when the health department came by for their inspection.

Even though he wasn't thinking about her, he did keep an ear out in case Lela decided to drop by, but she never did. His mood hadn't improved as he locked up for the night and made his solitary dinner.

Why would she write a suggestion in his notebook if she intended to make her own damn coffee? He fumed to his wolf.

I don't know. Why don't you go ask her? Sniff her out!

I'll do that, Jared thought, looking down at his dinner without much interest.

He ate the food and would have gone to bed early, but the alarm on his phone pinged, reminding him it was his turn to host card night. Cursing quietly, he quickly tidied and got out the cards and poker chips, grateful that the host didn't have to come up with the snacks.

. . .

Card night with some of the other shifters from Pinehurst was always a good way to socialize. The group was small, not too many people, and rarely included anyone Jared didn't already know, so Jared could skip the awkward small talk and the sharing of their life stories which strangers liked to indulge in all day at the Code Brew.

"Hey, is milk still making Caitlin sick?" Dakota Ford, one of the Pinehurst deputies, asked as he drew another card, signaling the end of his turn. "Sierra made homemade yogurt and she wanted her opinion."

"Yes," Owen, a part-time paramedic and deputy groaned. "It's awful. She gets so sad because she can't have any of her favorite things. Lela got her hooked on this coconut-based whipped cream stuff but Lizzie said it all got bought out and she's having trouble keeping it in stock. There's only one store in Red River that carries it and they said they are having the same issue."

"Yeah? That sucks," Dakota said.

The game ended later than Jared usually stayed up, but he didn't mind. They all cleaned up and said their goodbyes. When everyone was heading out, Jared stopped Owen with a word. Owen stepped back in and closed the apartment door.

"Hang on a sec, I have something for you. But you can't say you got it from me, and don't ask any questions."

"Okay..." Owen said, eyebrows lifting.

When Jared opened the fridge in the small kitchen, Owen blinked several times.

"I have to know," Owen said, his face incredulous as he stared at the contents of the fridge.

"I said don't ask questions."

"That isn't possible. What the hell are you doing with - how many cans of coconut whipped cream do you have in there?"

"Thirty-two."

"Thirty-two? What the hell. Are they for the shop?"

"Something like that," Jared said.

"Okay. I'll take a can. Thanks," Owen said, giving Jared a funny look.

"Here. Grab a bag," Jared said gruffly, indicating the grocery bag holder in one of the cabinets behind the counter.

Jared loaded him up with half a dozen cans for his pregnant mate.

"Jeez. What will I do with six of them?"

"Pregnant women love that shit. I bet she puts it on everything."

"So, you gonna tell me why you have these? The real reason?" Owen asked.

"Nope."

"Suit yourself. Night, and thanks. Caitlin thanks you too."

"Yup."

When Owen closed the door behind him, Jared locked up and got ready for bed.

You know, it's a lot of whipped cream, his wolf pointed out.

I'm running a coffee shop! Jared objected.

It's a specialty product. Did you buy the stores out just so she can't have any? His wolf asked, without judgement.

No. Of course not, Jared said, sighing. *Well, okay, maybe I did. Don't judge me.*

I was not judging you, his wolf sniffed. *I was going to say you need to steal the one from her office.*

I'm not doing that, Jared insisted.

Mmhmm, and meanwhile she's not going back to see us because she's got her can of of fancy special whipped cream over there in the chief's office. I bet she offers coffee to the first responders when they come in too. Really, she's taking away from your business, his wolf reasoned slyly. *You're just... helping the local economy by keeping your small business afloat.*

You're ridiculous, Jared thought back with a roll of his eyes as he readied himself for bed, and an early start in the morning.

Yeah, but if you do it you'll quit bitching all the time and you'll get to see her every morning again, maybe.

Maybe, Jared reasoned, just before falling asleep.

4

LELA

It wasn't often that she got off work late, but when the Chief worked long hours, Lela liked to stay and make sure he had what he needed. She was salaried, so she didn't need the money, but the Chief also had a tendency to leave a mess when he was alone in the office, and that made more work for her the next day. She preferred to come in first thing in the morning to a tidy office and a clearcut idea of what her daily tasks were, as much as possible.

This evening, she'd worked for two hours past her usual leaving time when she finally went home, bundled up in her heated coat with the battery pack that powered the heating element and kept her warm no matter how chilly it was outside.

"Hey, let me walk you?" one of the deputies, Scott said on her way out the door several weeks later. "It's getting dark."

"I'm walking six blocks straight down Main street," Lela laughed.

"Perfect. I'm going that way," Scott said as they walked right past his truck.

She let it go, knowing that if she didn't let him walk her, he would follow her in his truck to make sure she got home safe. That was one benefit to working in a small town with lots of shifter males: she always felt safe and protected.

"Okay."

"You want something? My treat," he offered, nodding his head toward Code Brew.

"Sure, although I should be treating you after the shift you all had."

"It was rough," he agreed, "But it's over now."

"You have any special plans tonight?" She asked as they walked, noting the moon on the rise.

"Nothing special, just looking for a little fun. How about you?"

"Oh, I have a hot date, this will be the third full moon in a row we've seen each other." She showed him a picture of her lock screen with her and three year old Jimmy.

"Nice," Scott said with a grin. "Kinda young."

"His mom and dad like to have someone in the house to listen out for him. He's a bit of a light sleeper, so they go to the motel on the full moon," Lela explained.

"Oh yeah, having a full moon with a light sleeper in the house wouldn't work for me."

They chuckled as they walked inside, Scott holding the door open for her.

"I'll have a large coffee, leave room for cream," Scott said.

"I'll have a slice of red velvet cake," she said, not meeting Jared's eye. She hadn't been in since he was so grumpy to her, and she almost felt bad about it.

"All out of red velvet, but I've got lemon," Jared said brusquely.

"Mm, that's okay. I'll have an iced decaf coffee."

"Sure thing," Jared replied.

She tried to pay for Scott's coffee, but he batted her hand away, giving her a look of amused rebuke.

"Absolutely not," he said, shaking his head. "Let's get you to your hot date, wouldn't want to keep the lucky fella waiting."

"Last time I was late he bit me. I was bruised for three days," she laughed as Scott handed her the coffee she ordered.

"Damn. That's harsh. Better make sure you aren't late. Night Jared!" Scott called as they headed out.

Lela noticed Jared scowling on her way back out the door, no surprise there. She was pleasantly surprised when she looked down and noticed that her coffee had snowflake sprinkles sitting on top of whipped cream.

When she put a finger down and tasted it, she realized it was the one she hadn't been able to find since she dropped her can and the tip broke off. She took a quick picture and made sure to tag Code Brew in it before heading to the Murphy's house to tuck Jimmy in of the night.

5

JARED

He was in a foul mood. After he locked up he got in the shower, the full moon making his entire body prickly and sensitive. Taking his cock in his fist, he stroked himself. When he closed his eyes, it wasn't his go-to fantasy he saw.

A pair of big brown eyes, long blonde hair, and slender hips filled his imagination. He imagined her kneeling in front of him in the shower, mouth open as water poured down, plastering her hair to her forehead. He wondered what color her nipples were as he imagined taking one in his mouth, sliding his fingers into her slippery pussy.

In his mind she had trimmed her hair, but not gone completely bald. Enough that he knew he was with a woman, but not so much that it would get in his way when he knelt at the end of his bed, pulling her to the edge of his mattress so he could make her his full moon dessert.

He hadn't been with a woman in so long, the idea of having a real flesh and blood fae like her in his shower and his bed, her lips wrapped around his cock had him spraying cum on the wall of the shower three times before the water started to get cold. He stood under the cold spray for a while, hoping the chilly water would take the edge off his arousal, but as soon as he stepped out into the steamy bathroom, his cock was hard again.

"Moon goddess," he cursed.

He dressed in the expensive athletic thermals he'd special ordered at a premium last year that bound magically to his human form, not shredding if he shifted to his wolf form clothed. Stepping outside, he shifted before going down the steps and headed toward the mountains, determined to run off his arousal, or at least exhaust himself so he could sleep.

HER EYES WERE red and puffy. Had her date gone badly, or had she been up all night fucking? He didn't like either option.

"Rough morning?" He asked her as she approached the counter.

"Yup. Same order as always, please," she replied, not looking up to meet his eye, sniffling. She pulled a tissue out of her pocket and dabbed at the corner of her eye.

"The day hasn't been long enough for it to be that bad yet."

"A branch came through my window last night during the storm. I was fine because I wasn't home, but my kitten got loose," she explained, eyes filling with tears.

He'd barely noticed the storm, he'd been so horny and irritated last night, but he'd seen the downed limbs and blown-in debris across Main street this morning when he'd come down to open up the shop.

"You have one of those chips in him?"

"His appointment was next week," she explained, tears spilling over as her lower lip trembled.

His muscles ached with the desire to put his arms around her and tell her everything would be fine.

What the fuck was wrong with him? He wasn't going to offer to hug her, that was just ridiculous. He didn't hug customers who were having a bad day. He gave them coffee and sent them on their way.

"I'm sure he'll come back. Cats are nothing if not annoyingly clingy."

"He's so little, he's still being bottle fed."

"He probably found somewhere nice and warm to hole up," When the morning rush died down Jared pulled out his phone.

"Zach, do you need some extra hours? I know it isn't your day to work, but I've had something come up." When Zach showed up, Jared headed for his apartment, changed into his thermals and phased into his wolf form.

Here, kitty kitty. His wolf's mental voice was lilted with humor. *This might be even more ridiculous than the whipped cream thing.*

What are you complaining about? You like tracking, Jared snapped at his wolf.

I like tracking prey, his wolf corrected. *I'm not a fucking collie.*

You didn't like the look on Lela's face anymore than I did, Jared countered.

Ah hah. Found her place! The wolf exclaimed, equally smug and excited.

He crawled up the branch, dropping carefully onto the floor. It was definitely her place. It smelled almost overwhelmingly of pine and cinnamon, mixed with her own unique scent.

Ooh, she smells nice. His wolf said in a heartily lustful tone.

Focus.

I'm focused! Just making an observation. I wonder what she'll say when we come home with her cat. I can think of a few ways she could thank us... His mind wandered into several scenarios with increasingly sexual overtones.

It took them six hours to find the little beast. By then, the ice had driven deep into his coat. He carried it carefully in his mouth to his apartment. He set it carefully in a cardboard box by the door so it didn't wander off while he phased back into human form.

Grumbling, he bundled the little thing inside of his coat and drove to the vet's office. The animal doc gave it a bottle and said it would be fine, just to keep it warm. Packing it back inside of his coat, he made his way to the admin building.

He knocked on her office door, but she wasn't in.

"You looking for Lela?" one of the girls from the office asked.

"Yeah, know where she is?"

"She's at the base, dealing with something with the Chief. Something I can help you with?"

"No thanks, I'll find her there."

He walked into the base, the kitten mewing pitifully in his coat. He patted it gently, shushing it. Proceeding back to the usually empty offices. She was bent over retrieving something off the floor, he took a moment to admire her figure. She straightened and he moved his eyes somewhere more socially appropriate.

"You scared me!"

"I have something for you," he said, pulling the kitten gingerly out of his coat.

"Legion!" she said, surging forward. "My baby."

"Legion?"

"Yeah. Like 'we are legion' - like a demon?"

He looked at the adorable fluffy bundle and raised an eyebrow, but she didn't notice, cuddling it to her chest.

"Where did you find him?" She asked.

"He was puttering around, happened to spot him while I was out. He wasn't with a momma and I figured there weren't that many lost kittens running around town."

He was pretty sure she wasn't listening, she'd cuddled inside of her shirt, unbuttoning the top button and settling the little bundle of fur onto her chest, nestled between her breasts.

That is one lucky kitty, his wolf leered as Jason rounded the corner.

"There's an apartment upstairs for you- what is that?" the chief said, narrowing his eyes suspiciously.

"Legion!" Lela volunteered

"Lela, I can't have a cat at the base," he said, his face looking disappointed that he couldn't tell her yes.

"What if I get my carrier and keep him in upstairs?" She asked hopefully.

"Sorry," Jason said, shaking his head with a look of regret in the kitten's direction.

"Okay. I'll figure it out."

"If you need to leave early to take him somewhere, do it now. I don't want any of my people out after dark in this weather," the Chief instructed.

"You sure, I can stay and-"

"Go, handle your cat issue. Text me updates of where you are, so I know you're safe."

The chief might just be her boss, and she might not be a shifter, but she responded to his order like she belonged to his pack. If Jared didn't know that his friend's interest was strictly a matter of making sure the people he was in charge of were safe and cared for, Jared would have been jealous.

"Yes sir," she said automatically.

I want her to say that to us, his wolf said.

Fucking hell. Shut the fuck up, Jared snapped, losing his cool.

I don't know why you're being shitty with me, his wolf snarked back. *I can hear your thoughts too, you know. You want her saying 'yes sir' as she submits to you as much as I want it. Why do you have your tail in a twist because I'm being honest about it?*

"Jared, you need something?"

"No, I was just coming by to drop off the hairball," he said.

When the chief had gone, she returned to stroking the kitten.

"Okay," she said to the kitten, "Let's see if we can find a couch to crash on. He's got to be fed, but I've got his bottles and stuff back at me apartment, I'll need to get that."

"He's still bottle-fed? How have you been taking care of him while you work?" Jared asked, trying not to be jealous of a kitten for where it was sitting against her warm skin.

"Yeah, he is. My neighbor across the hall keeps her during the day, she works from home, so I keep him after I'm home from work."

"Well, good luck."

"Thanks for stopping when you saw him."

"Yup."

When she came into the shop an hour later looking defeated as she ordered a hot coffee, he arched a brow.

"No luck?"

"No."

"You can stay upstairs if you want. It's close enough to work that you can some back and take care of him if you needed to."

"I couldn't do that," she said, but he wasn't willing to accept the look of tired defeat in her eyes.

"Doesn't seem like you have an alternative."

"They got the branch out of the living room and the hole is tarped now, so the apartment is safe to be in."

"You won't have any heat," he pointed out, not liking the idea of her staying somewhere that was just tarped over.

"I've got a heated blanket and a space heater in my bedroom," she said, looking at him significantly. He hadn't moved to make her drink and he started into action.

"There's no power," he informed her.

"What?"

"The whole complex is out," he informed her.

"Damn!"

"Stay with me, at least until the power comes back on."

"Um, thanks."

"Mmhmm. You have everything you need?"

She left and he thought about his place. He made up the couch for her, ignoring his wolf's suggestion that she would be more comfortable in their bed.

6

JARED

When a gentle knock came at his door he called for her to come in.

"Are you sure about this?" She asked when he'd invited her inside.

"Yup. The couch is all made up, the remote is there. Do you like lasagna?" Jared asked.

His wolf eagerly suggested they could go make something else if she wanted a different dinner.

"I love lasagna," she said, eyes sparkling with delight.

"Good, dinner will be ready in ten," he informed her, relieved that she'd looked genuinely pleased at his choice for their meal. He wasn't asking her to be his or anything, but the first meal a man fed a woman should be something she enjoys.

"Thanks, is there anything I can do?"

"No. Just set up your stuff and get comfy."

I wonder what she wears to bed.

Will you stop? Jared pleaded. He was just fine with his wolf not having thoughts about everything that he needed to share with Jared.

She's something worth talking about, his wolf said.

He was pulling the lasagna out of the oven when she came around into the small kitchen.

"Are you sure there isn't anything I can do?"

"You can set the table if you like. Plates are just there."

He turned on his true crime podcast out of habit, then turned it back off when he realized she might not like that.

"Ooh, that's a good episode," she said, eyes lighting up. "Have you listened to the one with the college campus stalker?"

They chatted easily through dinner about their favorite true crime cases. He disappeared to go shower, hoping if he relieved some of his sexual tension he could think straight. He found his release, but it felt hollow, and he just felt more irritated as he climbed out of the shower and got dressed in fresh clothing. When he came back out into the main room, she was nowhere to be found. The kitten was curled up in it's carrier, asleep, and he doubted Lela would just leave without saying anything, but the apartment wasn't that big. He stepped outside and breathed a sigh of relief.

She was standing in her coat, shivering, but staring out over the snow and ice-covered landscape.

"Why are you outside?" he asked, his voice gruff.

"Because it's snowing," she said in a hushed, reverent tone.

"And? Come back inside, it's too cold for a fae to be out here," he said, putting a hand on her arm.

"Just a sec. I needed this," she said softly, a single tear spilling down her cheek.

"Why?" He asked, looking at the pained expression on her face, wanting desperately to kiss it away.

"Do you know what it's like to remember a feeling?"

"Yes," he said, although he wasn't entirely sure he was, he wasn't going to break the moment by saying no.

"Snow makes me feel...whole. Safe. Like before."

He didn't press her, just waited for her to continue.

"I used to think all the magic in the world came from snow." She said. "It's easy to forget about snow when it's warm. Then things get cold and I feel like I'm always holding my breath, waiting for the next storm to come, waiting for the magic to come and blanket the world with sparkles."

"Hang on." He went inside and grabbed the warmest blanket he owned and came back outside. "Here."

He draped it around himself and enclosed her, trapping his body heat with hers. She drew closer to him, sighing happily.

"Now you can stay as long as you like," he said, his voice suddenly seeming too rough, too loud.

"I'm sure you have better things to do," she whispered, but she didn't move, holding her body still as his body heat warmed her.

"Nope."

Minutes past until he swore his feet were frozen, but he stayed where he was. He enjoyed the wholesome enjoyment she got, eyes sparkling as she admired the scene.

"I used to run to the window every morning it was cold to see if there was snow outside, to see if I could use my magic."

"Why aren't you using it now?"

"Cold is dangerous for us- for fae, I mean. One day I snuck out of the house to make a snow village. There was a castle with a draw-bridge. I was so intent on making it, I didn't realize how cold I was. When my parents found me I was half-dead. They decided it wasn't safe for me to have my magic anymore. The next day we went to see a doctor who put a permanent corundum implant inside of me, for my safety."

"Oh, Lela," he breathed, his heart breaking for her.

He didn't know what it was like to have magic abilities, but he could only imagine what it was like to have his wolf permanently silenced. His wolf whined at the thought and he pulled closer to Lela, trying to offer any comfort he could, even if it was only his body warmth.

"I remember being happy." She said softly. "That's what snow feels like. Happiness. The magic may be gone, but it still feels happy."

Something changed between them, like a line pulling their should together as he pulled her back tight against his chest.

"You deserve to be happy."

"I have glimpses of happiness. That's enough."

Jared's hand moved before he could think to stop himself. Reaching across her body he grabbed her shoulder and spun her around, taking one step forward so her back was pressed into the railing.

"You deserve to be happy, Lela. You deserve to have more than just fleeting moments of happiness." Then before he could stop to think about the consequences, he kissed her. She was a small dainty thing, all fae with her short build. Her height may have been short, but the soft curves of her hips that gave way beneath his rough grip turned him on. This was no girl, she was all woman - his woman.

He claimed her mouth, kissing her more fiercely when she stood on tiptoe to meet him, one small hand sliding up his chest. He only broke the kiss to stop and pick her up, bringing her inside so hhe could carry her to his bed.

"Jared," she said in a small voice when his set her down, kneeling before her to unlace her shoes, removing them carefully.

"Hm?" He asked.

"What are you doing?"

"Showing you how much happiness and pleasure you deserve."

Uncertainty crossed her face. He frowned. "You deserve as much happiness as this world can give you."

He stripped his shirt off, tossing it neatly into the laundry basket in the corner, then he undressed her with slow, deliberate care.

7

LELA

He was so gentle, so tender, that she didn't want to interrupt the moment.

She did not want to tell this virile, sexy man that she'd never had sex before.

"Touch yourself, baby. Show me how you make yourself feel good," he took her hand and placed it near her, thankfully, freshly shaved lower regions.

Her cheeks promptly flamed and she closed her fingers, trying to find the words to tell him she hadn't ever done that.

"Don't be embarrassed," he said, leaning down to place a kiss on the inside of her thigh.

"Please, don't make me," she whispered.

He looked up, his eyes sweeping over her and he shook his head.

"Of course, I won't make you," he said. His eyes softened as he looked at her face. "Lela, do you need me to be in charge? To just do things to you and make you submit to me? Is that what you need?"

She nodded, relieved. That was exactly what she wanted. She didn't want to do it wrong, she was sure someone like him had taken plenty of girls to bed and knew how to do all the right things. She didn't want him to be irritated if she wasn't good, but if he was in charge, he would tell her exactly how he wanted it, so she could be good for him, too.

"Okay, I can do that. You know about safe words?"

She nodded.

"Tell me out loud. If you know about safe words, you say 'Yes, sir' for me."

"Yes sir, I do."

"Good girl," he praised, moving between her legs.

He knelt between her legs and just stared for a moment, running his fingers through her landing strip.

"You're so beautiful," he breathed, his mouth so close to hers that she felt his hot breath on her... down *there.*

He leaned forward, closing the distance between his mouth and her privates and his tongue swiped, beginning at her entrance and ending at her clit, where she'd only ever used a vibrator to play with herself.

"I can't wait to have my cock buried in you any longer," he groaned, stopping before her orgasm had completely faded.

She should tell him. Gathering her courage as she took a deep breath in, she started to confess.

"Jared, I haven't-"

"I'm clean," he said. "I haven't been with anyone in a long time, but I've been tested. Do you want me to get a condom?"

"No," she breathed, all her courage evaporating, anticipation rising in her chest.

She didn't know much, but she couldn't get pregnant because of her implant, and she wanted to feel everything about her first time.

"You're sure?"

"Yes, I'm sure. I'm definitely clean."

He positioned himself at her entrance, his eyes sliding closed as he slid just the tip in.

"You're so tense," he murmured, pushing in just a little, and leaning forward to kiss her. "Relax, baby. Let me in, and I'll make you feel so good."

"Yes sir," she replied, trying to relax.

"Just like that," he groaned as he inched forward, withdrawing a little, then pulling back before pressing back inside of her, each time getting a little deeper. "Let me in, my good girl."

"Jared," she panted, anxious to have the worst part over.

"Yes, baby?"

"Stop being so gentle, please," she begged.

"You want it hard?" he paused.

"Yes, sir."

He withdrew, rubbing his cock on her clit for a moment, driving her wild until she started to orgasm. Just as she cried out, he moved and with one smooth motion, drove his cock deep inside of her, forcing her body to accept his entire length. She cried out, clawing at his chest and neck, half-wanting him to stop, but also desperate for him to keep going.

"Spread your legs for me, let me see this pretty pussy as I fuck you," he said, his voice going deep and ragged as he held her legs behind her knees, staying deep inside of her, barely withdrawing before he surged forward, driving him deeper than before.

"Don't move, baby, or you're going to make me come," he warned.

But her whole body was on fire, stretched and tender, but desperate to find another release with something inside of her. She moved slightly. He closed his eyes with a primal groan, his hips thrusting forward as his warmth flooded her and he worked his cock deep inside of her.

"Holy moon, baby."

He kissed her, staying inside of her while she joined him in her release, her insides contracting and gripping his cock.

"That was perfect," he praised. "Good girl. Now, I want to see what you taste like with my cum inside of you."

He moved away from her, glancing down and noting the blood on his shaft.

"Sweetheart, you're bleeding, are you expecting your period?" he asked, looking concerned as he lifted his eyes from hers

"I think that's normal the first time," she said, her eyes flicking briefly to his cock, but they flew to his face when he uttered a curse.

"Your first time? You're a virgin?" He demanded. Sitting back on his haunches, he drew his hand through his hair.

"FUCK!"

8

JARED

Immediately, her eyes flooded with tears and he cursed again.

"No, no, sweetheart, come here," he said, moving around on the bed.

"I'm sorry-" she said in a small voice through her tears.

"Stop," he commanded. "You listen to me. You were perfect, everything you did was perfect. Your body, your noises, how you look and smell and feel, every bit of it was perfect."

"You're mad."

"Yeah, I am," he admitted. "But I'm not mad at you. I just had no idea, I thought when you said your last partner on the full moon bit you that you were- that you'd been with people."

She laughed a little, wiping her tears away.

"I babysit on the full moon, so parents can enjoy it without worrying about their kids overhearing them in the middle of a rut."

"Oh," he said, relief flooding him at the realization that she hadn't been with anyone else.

He tried to convince himself that it was fine if she had been, but the knowledge that she'd only been with him made his chest swell.

"I'm sorry," she repeated.

"Stop, or I'll spank you," he said. "I'm not mad at you. I'm mad at myself for not stopping to have a conversation before I drug a virgin into my bed and asked you if you wanted me to dominate you while I forcefully took your virginity. Oh moon, I'm the one who's sorry."

Guilt rolled through him, until his eyes met hers and she offered a small, shy smile.

"I really liked it," she admitted, her cheeks blazing.

He sighed as his wolf gave a rumble of pleasure, and offered a suggestion of what else they could do for her that she might enjoy.

"Can we do it more?"

He groaned as his cock began to harden again and he climbed on top of her.

"Anything you want," he said.

"Anything?" she teased.

"Anything," he repeated.

"Even my coconut whipped cream?" her eyes sparkled with merriment.

He looked down at her for a moment, then got up out of the bed, taking her hand and pulling her to her feet.

"What-"

"Sh," he commanded, pulling her into his kitchen and opening the fridge.

Her eyes widened.

"You- bought them all?"

"I wanted you to come back," he said gruffly.

She turned to look at him, half-indignant, half laughing at him.

"You're kind of a dick," she pointed out.

"Yeah, so I've been told." He grinned at her, then knelt down and took her hand.

"Would you do me the honor of allowing me to claim you, Lela?"

"Only if there are snowflake sprinkles, too," she said, smiling up at him.

He grunted and stood, flicking open the cabinet behind her, then spinning her around. There, with her name written in his neat print, was a jar of snowflake sprinkles.

"In that case, you're all mine, now," he said, putting a hand on her back to push her forward, bending her over the counter and readying himself to take her again.

THE END

Printed in Great Britain
by Amazon